FIRST COMES HARRY

Written and Illustrated by Taro Gomi

EARLY BIRD COLLECTION AUTHORS

John McInnes, *Senior Author*   Glen Dixon   John Ryckman

early bird

PUBLISHED SIMULTANEOUSLY IN 1990 BY:

Nelson Canada,
A Division of International
Thomson Limited
1120 Birchmount Road
Scarborough, Ontario   M1K 5G4

AND

Delmar Publishers Inc.,
A Division of Thomson Corp.
2 Computer Drive, West
Box 15015
Albany, NY 12212-5015

**Canadian Cataloguing
in Publication Data**

Gomi, Taro.
  First comes Harry

(Early bird collection)
ISBN 0-17-603027-1

I. Title.   II. Series.

PZ7.G586Fi   1990   j895.6'35   C89-095093-8

**Library of Congress
Cataloging-in-Publication Data**

Gomi, Taro.
  First comes Harry.

  (Early bird)
  Translation of: Ichiban Hajimeni.
  Summary: Harry has a busy day, always being
the first in such activities as waking up, eating
breakfast, going outside, playing, and getting
ready for bed.
    I. Title.   II. Series: Early bird (Albany, N.Y.)
PZ7-G586Fi   1980   [E]   89-23351
ISBN 0-8273-4124-5

Text and illustrations copyright © 1984 by Taro Gomi
Originally published in 1984 in Japanese, under the title *Ichiban Hajimeni*,
by Kaisei-sha Publishing Co., Ltd.

English translation rights arranged with Kaisei-sha Publishing Co., Ltd., through
Japan Foreign-Rights Centre. Reprinted by arrangement with Morrow Junior Books,
A Division of William Morrow & Company, Inc.

Co-ordinating Editor: Jean Stinson
Project Manager: Jocelyn Van Huyse-Wilson
Editor: Irene Cox
Art Director: Lorraine Tuson
Series Design and Art Direction: Rob McPhail
Typesetting: Trigraph Inc.
1 2 3 4 5 6 7 8 9 0 EB 9 8 7 6 5 4 3 2 1 0

Harry woke up first.

Then the dog woke up.

The cat was sleeping...

and so was the baby.

Father and Mother were sleeping, too.

Harry got dressed first...

and brushed his teeth first.

He was the first to sit down at the table...

and the first to eat all his breakfast.

He was the first to go outside.

The dog went along.

Harry was the first to jump over the trash can...

the first to race up the slide...

and the first to tumble down the slide.

Ouch!

He was the first to laugh...

and the first to shout...

the first to march...

the first to stand on his head. . .

and the first to see an airplane in the sky.

Harry was the first to go home...

the first to jump into the bathtub...

and the first to feel sleepy.

Good night.